The Three Cousins and the Bank Heist

John Riley

with

Evelyn Adams

Other books by John Riley

The Heifers Save Christmas

I love This Farm

The author would like to thank Evelyn Adams for her ideas and help in outlining the book. Without her enthusiasm and encouragement this project wouldn't have been started. I have enjoyed every minute of working with her and extend my best wishes for success in her future endeavors.

A big thank-you to Pam Rogers for the offer to proof read and make suggestions. Her hard work has proved invaluable in making this book better.

This is a work of fiction. All of the characters, organizations, locations, and events portrayed in this novel are either the product of the author's wild imagination or are used fictitiously.

Chapter One

Camp Out

"What are those birds doing?" Eli lay on his back and pointed to the sky. Above him, barn swallows wheeled and dove in the late evening sky. The sun was a disappearing red-orange ball to the west. Eli and his twelve-year-old cousin, Evy, and his seven-year-old sister, Sami, lay on their backs on a blanket and watched the sun go down. The high hill in the middle of the hay field next to their grandparent's farmhouse provided a panoramic view of the surrounding farm land. Eleven-year-old Eli's grandparents lay on another blanket next to the children.

"They are catching insects," Grandma replied. "Watch how they do acrobatics to catch the bugs in the air," she pointed. At that moment a large bird flashed by overhead.

"A night hawk," Grandpa said. "I don't know if that's really the name of the bird, but that's what I call it," he added. "It's catching insects, too."

The birds put on an air show high above. The family lay on the blankets and watched.

"Look at the sky," Sami said. "It's dark above us, and it turns lighter blue to the west, and then it is pink and red at the sunset." She propped up on one elbow and glanced around.

"It will be dark soon," Grandpa said. "You kids will want to take your showers and head for the camper."

"Can't we stay out a little longer?" dark haired Evy pleaded. "I love watching the sunset, and then the world turns to night."

"We do have a little longer," Grandma replied. "It certainly is peaceful, isn't it?"

The others agreed and laid back to watch as the sky darkened and the birds disappeared one by one. To the excitement of the children, a bat fluttered overhead. Crickets began to chirp in the grass along the fence line behind them. High in the darkening sky above them, the first star silently peaked out. Grandma stood up. "Time to go in," she stated. The others reluctantly stood, their grandfather somewhat stiffly, and folded their blankets.

After trekking to the house, the children

showered and headed to the motor home parked in the front yard. The cousins soon settled in for the night as their grandparents went to the house. While Sami fell into a deep slumber, Evy and Eli read comic books for a while before turning out the lights. They drifted off to sleep, unaware of earlier developments to the east.

Chapter Two

Deception!

Two men leaped into the waiting car. One in the back, the other in the front passenger seat. A man sat waiting behind the wheel. The man in the front turned to the driver. "Step on it Slim!" he commanded in a rough voice.

Slim was already reaching down and slipping the car into drive. Glancing over his left shoulder, he eased into traffic. The man in the front seat turned to the back and dropped a small cloth bag and a rectangular tin box on the floor. "Cover that up, Rocky," he said.

Rocky was in the middle of removing a fake mustache. He finished, then reached down and placed a brown blanket on the floor opposite him. He smiled back at the front seat passengers.

"We pulled it off, boys," he said.

"We ain't in the clear yet," the man, who was obviously the boss, replied. He looked at Slim again. "I said, step on it, you fool. The bank is going to figure out we're fakes and call in the cops."

Slim said, "We blend in better by following traffic rules. No need to call attention to ourselves by speeding. Look around," he continued. "See all the silver cars? That's why I rented this silver Toyota. We fit right in. Seems like everybody in Ann

Arbor, or nearly everybody, drives a silver Toyota of some sort." He grinned over at his passengers. "Besides, it's rush hour. We'll be hard to spot in this five o'clock traffic. We'll get lost in the crowd then head outta' town."

"Yeah, Jocko," came Rocky's voice from the back seat. "We got nothin' to worry about. We got the cash and jewels from the house and the real valuable stuff from the deposit box at the bank. They won't figure it out 'til somebody checks it. That could be months from now. You know how those rich people are. Got more money than they can keep track of." He shifted in his seat and reached across into a paper bag laying on the seat beside him.

"You can thank me for getting my hands on the key and the bank papers," put in Slim. He was eyeing traffic around them as he slowed the Toyota and made a right-hand turn.

11

Rocky twisted the cap from a plastic water bottle and took a long drink. He reached into the bag beside him and, pulling out another bottle, handed it over the seat-back to Jocko. "You want one?" he asked Slim.

"Naw, I had a coffee earlier. Any more liquids and I'll have to stop by the side of the road," Slim said.

Rocky settled back and sipped his water. He looked out the window absentmindedly.

A black and white police cruiser was parked at the side of the street. It slipped into traffic a few cars back and followed behind, the driver keeping his distance. Slim sucked in his breath.

Jocko said some words under his breath that even burglars and thieves shouldn't say.

Slim changed to the left lane, being careful to signal his maneuver beforehand.

Several cars back, the black and white

signaled and changed lanes behind them.

"Coincidence," said Slim with a glance in the rear-view mirror and a slight edge of worry in his voice. He slowed the car and stopped in the line for the left-turn lane. Traffic was still heavy and when the left-turn arrow switched to green, the Toyota was the last one through before the light turned red again.

Slim made the turn onto westbound Jackson Street and crowded the speed limit as he sought to put more distance between the cop car and theirs. Checking the rear-view mirror again, he noticed the police car turn the corner. There was enough traffic between the two cars that Slim was able to cut down a side street and doubled back. In the back seat, Rocky peered out the rear window to watch for the police car.

Slim turned and drove south a few blocks

then turned right again. "I've got our switch waiting for us a little way over," he stated. He drove through a quiet residential neighborhood a few blocks off the business district. At a quiet intersection he turned right, heading north until he turned again, this time into a back lot of a car dealership. There were no people or car traffic in the back lot. Pulling in next to a newer, blue, four-door Impala, he switched off the Toyota. "This is it," he stated firmly. Pulling a set of keys from his pocket, he hit the buttons to release the trunk of the Impala and to unlock the doors. Turning to Jocko, he handed both sets to him.

"Hurry up, before the cops show up," Jocko muttered as he dropped the cloth bag and tin box into the trunk. He started to walk away, thought better of it, and returned to the trunk and slipped the items down in the well around the spare tire. He then stood up and, taking the keys to the Toyota from his pocket, gave them a toss.

Slim handed his partners a paper bag containing a change of clothes each, slid into the back seat and, slumping down, closed his eyes. "Wake me when we're in Battle Creek," he muttered.

Jocko slid behind the wheel, with Rocky riding shotgun. Jocko was glad to see the Impala had a full tank of gas. Slim had done his job well. Not only was it Slim who found the mark while working as a gardener and handyman, he'd "borrowed" the key and papers necessary to get them into the bank security boxes. It was Slim who had the fake identification made for Jocko to sign in at the bank. At this point Jocko stripped off his own fake goatee, a Van Dyke, and handed it to Rocky. "Put this in the glove box 'til I can

15

ditch it," Jocko told him. Rocky complied.

Jocko drove the Impala a few blocks to a busy corner and pulled into the parking lot of a service station convenience store. "We've got to get out of these clothes," he said to Rocky. Jocko parked the Impala close to the outside restrooms and took the paper bag containing the change of clothing in with him. He emerged in minutes wearing blue jeans and a brown plaid shirt with the sleeves rolled up. "Make it fast," he said to Rocky, flinging the bag across the seat. Rocky grabbed it up and headed to the men's room.

"Don't I even have time for a cold pop?" he queried over his shoulder.

"No," came Jocko's harsh reply. "We'll stop later. This place could be crawling with cops pretty soon, and you want to dilly-dally." He muttered some more under his breath.

Rocky emerged shortly. He was wearing a red polo shirt, blue jeans, and was sporting a much shorter hair style.

"What'd you do with the wig?" Jocko asked as Rocky climbed into the car.

"In the trash, along with our old clothes," responded Rocky. "I dumped your stuff in there, too."

"Better hope no snoopy cop finds it," growled Jocko as he glanced around and backed the car from the parking spot.

From the back seat came the sound of light snoring.

Jocko drove the car north and turned westbound again onto Jackson Street. The Impala was soon taking the entrance ramp to I-94 westbound. "So far, so good," Rocky looked behind them.

"Now if Slim has the next switch waiting and a place to hang out, we'll be alright,"

Jocko breathed a sigh of relief. He glanced into the rear-view mirror at Slim sleeping soundly in the back seat, and smiled.

"We'll be able to buy all the clothes we'll need," laughed Rocky.

"That we will," said Jocko with a broad smile. He held his hand up to Rocky for a high five. The car merged into the right lane and sped down the highway.

Chapter three

Discovery

Something just didn't add up for the vault
security manager. He had a funny feeling
about the pair ever since they came into the
vault area. Finally yielding to his
suspicions, he went to his office, looked up a
phone number and placed a call to the owner of
the safety deposit box. He asked if the owner
had authorized anyone to examine the box, or

if he himself had been in within the past half-hour.

"No," replied the owner. "My rare coin collection is in there along with some of my wife's grandmother's jewelry. There are also a few stock certificates, payable to bearer of course." There was worry in his voice. "The key and paperwork are in the safe in my study. I'll check to see if they're missing."

He was absent only for a minute when he returned abruptly. "Gone!" he exclaimed. "I've been robbed!"

The head of security assured the customer that he would summon the police, and requested the man to come to the bank as soon as possible. They would need a detailed list of the contents of the safety deposit box.

The security manager returned to the safety deposit vault and, upon examining the log, asked to speak with the clerk who had conducted the session.

"There were two men," responded the clerk. One was taller than the other. The short one had sort of a short afro type hair style, brown in color. The taller one had brown hair, too. Nothing special. Medium length. And he wore a Van Dyke beard. You know, just on his chin. Don't see too many of them around, but this is Ann Arbor after all," he said with a shrug. The security man nodded his understanding.

"The other man, the short one, had a mustache. It was brown, too, but not the same shade as his hair. I wondered if the mustache was a fake when I saw it. That's what made me call you. They had the key and proper papers of authorization," he added. "And the tall guy presented a driver's license with picture I.D.

"We've pulled the tapes," stated the

security man. "We'll get a good look at these guys when we review them."

At this point a police detective and two uniformed officers were escorted in. The clerk repeated his story and walked the officers to the front door of the bank, where a security guard led them to the sidewalk and pointed in the direction in which the men had gone. As they talked, a college student walked up.

"Excuse me, officers," the young man said. "I couldn't help but hear part of your conversation. When I walked up to the bank a little while ago, two men matching the description you've been mentioning walked by me. They walked quickly and had the look of trouble about them."

"The look of trouble?" asked the detective. "How would you know that?"

"My dad's a cop in Indianapolis," the

young man replied, "and so is my uncle. My grandfather is a retired cop. We know what to keep our eyes open for."

"Good for you, son," replied the bank security officer. "Now, did you see if they kept walking, or turned off?"

"Even better," replied the student with a smile. "I saw the car they got into. They were about three blocks from the bank. One, the shorter one, bumped my shoulder as he passed on the sidewalk. I turned to watch them. They just seemed odd to me. That's when they left the sidewalk and got into a newer, silver Toyota four door. A man behind the wheel was waiting for them, with the engine running. There was a sticker on the back of the car, on the trunk lid."

"A sticker?" the police asked in unison.

"Yes, a rental car sticker." And the student divulged the name of the company on the sticker.

"Michigan plate," added the student. "I got the first three numbers. Then they were gone into traffic."

"Would you like a job?" the detective asked, laughing. He wrote down what the young man had to tell him and got on his cell phone to call in the information. "There must be hundreds of silver cars in Ann Arbor," he said, turning back to the group. "I wonder how many are Toyotas?"

"They've got just over an hour start on us," offered the bank security manager. "They could be in Detroit already. Or Toledo," he added glumly.

"Might still be in town for that matter," replied one of the uniformed officers.

"They'll probably wait to make sure the heat is off and then take off, if they haven't already hit the freeway," offered the college student. "But I'd ditch the car first if it were me," he added with a slight shrug.

The detective whipped out his phone again while eyeing the student. "Yeah, Bennett here. Have your boys look for a silver Toyota four-door that's been abandoned somewhere. Probably off the beaten path. Yes, the same one I called in the partial plate on. Sure, anytime," and he hung up.

He handed the student his business card with a broad grin on his face. "Give me a call," he said. "I'd like to talk some more." He slapped the young man on the back and turned away. His cell phone rang and he jerked it to his ear. "Yes?" Listening for a moment he turned to the student. Holding his hand over the phone he called out. "Bingo! We got a hit on a silver Toyota on the back lot of a car dealership out on West Jackson Road." He shook his head and grinned again. And pointing at the student, "You'd better call me."

"Will do."

The uniformed men shook their heads and chuckled to themselves.

At the back lot of the car dealership, officers stood in a group around two technicians as they dusted the car for prints. The doors were locked and the keys nowhere to be found.

"We pretty sure this is the car?" asked Bennett as he walked up to the group. He stepped behind the car and read the name of the rental company on the sticker. Pulling out his note pad, he compared the first three digits on the plate with those that the student had given him earlier. He smiled and gave a satisfied grunt. "This is it, boys," he stated.

"Locked with no keys, detective," one of

the officers stepped forward. "We can try and jimmy the door," he said.

Bennett said, "Let's look around for the keys, first." He gazed down and the officers began searching the area.

"Anybody see who left the car, and what they took off in?" asked Bennett. He was eyeing two boys who sat straddling their bicycles on the sidewalk. Bennett walked over.

"There been a murder?" one of the boys asked, his eyes wide in wonder.

"Naw," replied the detective and he introduced himself. "Just a lost car for now. You boys see anything?"

"Well," replied the smaller of the boys, "three men pulled up in the little car. They left in a blue car, a bigger car."

Bennett took him to be the bigger kid's brother due to their close resemblance,

"A Toyota?" asked the detective.

"Nope, a Chevy," replied the older of the boys. "An Impala four-door. Our stepdad's got one just like it, 'cept it's black. He don't drive nothin' but Chevies."

The little kid said, "The bigger guy threw the keys to the little car over there." He pointed to some nearby bushes, then added, "He said bad words and wasn't nice to the other two guys."

Following the boy's direction, an officer walked over and peered into the bushes. He moved the grass around with his shoe, then stooped to pick something up. Turning triumphantly, he held the keys up for all to see, then walked over to the Toyota.

Chapter Four

The Getaway

Mixed in with the heavy traffic, the blue Impala headed west. Jocko used his mirrors to keep an eye out for police cruisers. Near the Zeeb Road overpass he spotted a State Police car parked at the top of the entrance ramp. Jocko forced his way out into the traffic flow of the left lane and got beside an eighteen wheeler. He slowed to stay beside the truck until well past the interchange, hidden from

the patrol car. Traffic backed up behind him.
Finally he pulled in front of the truck as
cars whizzed by. He mumbled some more harsh
words about speeders and set his cruise on
seventy.

"That state cop makes me nervous," he said
to Rocky. "And I just saw another one heading
east-bound."

"They could be on to us," remarked Rocky
with concern. "Maybe we should split up. You
know, until things cool off."

"I'll jump over to old Michigan Ave.
There's a train station in Jackson. Slim
doesn't know it yet, but he's going for a
ride." Then he added with a sideways glance
at Rocky, "We'll keep the loot with us."

"We switched cars," complained Rocky.
"How could we be suspect? Even if they found
the Toyota."

"I don't know what kind of trail Slim

left," Jocko replied, while glancing in the rear-view mirror. "Hey, Slim. Wake up," he bellowed. "Could the cops know what we're driving?"

Slim roused himself from his nap in the back seat. "What's the deal here," he groused. "Naw, they couldn't have traced us. Unless..." and his voice trailed off for a moment. "Unless somebody spotted us making the switch. But they wouldn't think anything of it unless the cops started sniffing around." He made a sour face. "I knew I should have parked this car at the park and ride. I just didn't want it to sit for a long time and arouse suspicion. Next time, that's what I'll do," he added thoughtfully.

"Next time?" snorted Jocko. "Oh brother!" and he glanced over at Rocky. "They can't trace the rental, can they?" he asked pointedly. The car was now on the exit and slowing for the stop sign at the bottom of the ramp.

"I used a fake I.D.," Slim replied. "If they're looking for three guys in a blue Impala, then we'll get us another car. This one's not stolen, so it's not on the hot sheet. I leased it for two years from GM," and he gave a snort of laughter.

As the three drove west on Michigan Avenue toward the town of Grass Lake, Jocko explained his plan to Slim.

Slim didn't particularly like it, but he didn't protest either. "There's a car dealership on the left up here," he said. It's not too late to make another switch.

Jocko drove on.

Within twenty minutes they were in Jackson and following old Michigan Avenue, were nearing downtown. The train station was on their left. A sign announced that the building was on the National Registry of Historical Sites. Jocko pulled in and parked the Impala in front of the tidy, well-kept, brick building. He walked in with Slim and checked the schedule. The eight-o'clock train was due in forty-five minutes. The friendly clerk said it wasn't running late. Jocko left Slim looking over the restored interior of the building and returned to the car. Following Slim's instructions, he drove a block to Cooper and headed north to the I-94 interchange.

Chapter Five

Midnight Walk

"Sami? Sami, you awake?"

Sami roused herself from her sleep. Her cousin Evy was gently rocking her shoulder. Her brother, Eli, peered over Evy's shoulder. He wore a wide grin and held a flashlight in his hand.

"What's up? Can't you guys let a person sleep?" Sami groused. "It must be the middle of the night." She sat up and rubbed her eyes.

"Just past midnight, actually." Evy stepped back as Sami tossed back her blanket and swung her legs over the side of the bed in the motor home.

Sami looked at them both. "Grandpa said we weren't supposed to go running around all night, or we couldn't sleep in the camper," she said.

"We're just going for a walk in the whispery woods," Evy replied. Being the eldest of the three cousins, Evy was usually the instigator in their adventures.

"Especially back in the woods," Sami retorted.

"I've got my flashlight." Eli switched it on and waved it at her.

"Let me put my shoes on," little Sami replied sourly. "Are we taking the dog?" She glanced under the table across from her at the border collie. The dog's tail thumped rhythmically as their eyes met.

"We can't go without Candy," Eli said. "What if we run into a coyote, or something worse?"

Sami finished slipping into her farm boots and stood up. "Do I get a flashlight, too?"

Evy produced a small mag light and handed it over. "Let's go," she directed, and she turned to open the screen door. Candy, the farm dog, forced her way ahead of the children and leaped to the ground. Eli carefully closed the screen behind them, and the children walked across the dark yard and across the gravel drive to the lane. Evy opened a gate just far enough for the three to squeeze through. Eli came through last, shouldered the gate closed and latched the security chain.

They came to the large, round, cow tank.

Eli shined his light into the tank, only to have it reflect off the water and cast eerie shadows on the trees near them. He changed the angle of the beam and soon all three were peering into the depths of the water, watching tadpoles swim about. Eli plunged his free arm in. "Almost caught one!" he exclaimed.

"Shh," cautioned Evy. "We don't want to wake anyone up.

"Look," Sami said, none too quietly herself, "there are the goldfish Grandpa put in," she pointed out. "They're swimming around with the tadpoles."

Each year, for some unexplained reason, there were tadpoles in the cow tank. Everyone figured that tree frogs lay eggs in there during the spring, but the tadpoles were present all summer long. Some were large and others small. The children never saw one actually develop legs. The tadpoles, or polliwogs as some called them, were frequently spotted nibbling at algae growth on the tank sides. The kids loved to catch them and then release them back into the tank. Then, in late spring, their grandfather had placed a half-dozen goldfish in the tank to control the mosquito wrigglers. The goldfish coexisted with the tadpoles all summer.

Sami stood with her arms thrust into the water up to her elbows, her flashlight held between her teeth. She came up with her hands cupped and a large tadpole wriggling frantically in her palms. She started to say something, but the mag light fell from her mouth as she spoke. Evy quickly snatched up the light before it reached the water. Sami released the tadpole and took the light back as Evy made clucking noises to herself and slowly shook her head.

A warm, southerly breeze sprang up and

brought the moist smells of late spring from the fields and the woods to the cousins.

"Let's go see if the creek is still running," suggested Eli. "We could wade in it through the woods." He directed his light down the path. The three cousins stood looking at each other.

"I dare you to go first," Sami said to Eli.

"I'm not scared," he replied, nervously taking a few steps forward.

Candy, the farm dog, raced ahead. She held her tail up like a bushy flag, nose working the breeze. Eli followed with his light. Evy and Sami looked at each other and hurried to catch up. To their right, over the lane fence, was a freshly planted field. The children had helped pick stones two weeks earlier to prepare for the corn planting.

Abruptly, Evy switched off her light.

Looking skyward she exclaimed, "Look at all the stars!"

Eli turned to face her, switching off his own light. Sami put her hand over her lens and looked up, too. The sky seemed to be scattered with bright jewels. Pinpoints of light spread above the world as far as the eye could see.

"We're lucky to not have street lights out here," Evy said. "We can even see planets." She pointed to the west at a very bright star-looking object. "I think it's Mars or Venus," she said. Grandpa told me about it.

Sami uncovered her lens and said, "Let's go. I'm getting tired."

"Let's go in the woods first," Evy urged. "Maybe we'll find an animal. Maybe even a raccoon."

"Or a skunk!" hoped Eli.

Candy growled low in her throat; a playful

soft growl, and dashed ahead. The dog looked intently up a tree, her tail thrashing in enjoyment.

"She's found something!" Eli exclaimed.

Evy walked briskly ahead. "Good girl," she said, reaching down to pat Candy's head.

Eli and Sami joined her. They aimed their lights a short way up the trunk of the wild cherry tree. Piercing eyes of glowing coals reflected back at them. "What is it? Is it a woods monster?" Sami asked nervously. "Or a swamp monster? I knew we shouldn't have come back here!"

"The barn is fifty feet away," Evy replied in annoyance. "Everybody knows that swamp monsters don't go near barns or houses. They're too scared." She tried to sound brave, but wasn't all too sure, herself.

Evy directed her light up the tree to combine her beam with Eli's and Sami's.

41

"Puff," she exclaimed. "It's only Puff. You gave us a scare old boy."

"Here kitty, kitty," Sami called in a worried tone.

"Let's go," Eli said. "He'll come down by himself when he's good and ready." He turned his back on the cat. Reluctantly, Sami followed the two down the farm lane. Candy, the farm dog, ran ahead a few paces and led the way. The breeze continued from the south, causing the trees to sway and groan, and bringing night noises from the woods. Candy stopped. Her ears pricked up and she growled again deep in her throat. Not a friendly, soft growl like she gave her friend, Puff, the cat, but a sound that was a warning from within. Her nose and ears worked the breeze. She heard something that the cousins did not.

"What is it girl?" Sami asked, while resting her hand on Candy's back.

"Easy, girl," Evy added. We don't want to wake up the neighborhood or scare off a deer or something." Evy knew that with the nearest neighbor a quarter mile away, there would be no waking anyone.

Candy walked ahead, her nose and ears busy on the breeze. The children passed through an open gate and into the woods. "I'll bet it's only the cattle," Eli whispered bravely.

"Cattle don't get her stirred up," Sami replied. "It must be some other animal."

The children followed a well-worn cow path that wound its way through the woods. The woods itself took on an eerie personality in the middle of the night. "It's like being in a huge room populated by trees," Evy spoke nervously. "Only, the roof is so high up... and painted with glowing stars."

They walked quietly now, crowded together on the trail, as Candy led the way. Presently the dog stopped. Low noises came from deep in her throat again. The hackles stood up on her back.

Evy thought she heard a far off voice. "A radio?" she wondered half aloud to herself. But then she heard it again.

"Hear that?" Eli whispered. "It's coming from the back of the woods, near the road." An east-west road ran along the back of the farm.

"I thought I heard something," Evy answered.

"Me, too," replied Sami. "I thought somebody left a radio on."

"So did I, at first," answered Evy. "Only there are no radios back here. Even with the way sound travels at night, I don't think we'd hear something from the next block over. And it's a voice - not singing, music, or complete sentences. The wind is mixing it up."

The children followed Candy along the path through the trees. Coming to a fence, they took turns helping each other step through. They heard the sound again. Evy put her hand on Candy's collar to silence her low growling.

"Look!" Eli pointed through the trees. "I saw a light flash." He spoke urgently, in a voice just above a whisper.

The girls looked. Sami crowded closer to Evy. Candy stared intently.

Chapter Six

The Heat Is On!

Jocko and Rocky had proceeded west of
Jackson on I-94. At the Dearing Road
interchange a State Police car was parked near
the top of the east-bound exit ramp. An
officer had the driver's door open and stood
between the door and the car, scanning the
traffic on the freeway. He didn't bother with
a radar gun. He was clearly looking for
something, or someone, in particular.

"Another one," Jocko groused, more to himself than to anyone. In his side mirror he watched as the officer got into the patrol car and edged up the exit ramp to the cross-road and disappeared.

"Think he's coming after us?" Rocky asked nervously. He paled slightly. "I bet he's coming to pull us over."

"We're going to play it safe," Jocko responded. The next exit, we're going to get off and let things cool down. Man, I wish Slim were here. He'd have this figured out. Guess I shouldn't have ditched him in Jackson."

The state patrol car didn't appear in the rear-view mirror as the blue Impala sped along. Within minutes they arrived at Exit 130. Jocko turned on his directional signal to exit the freeway. At the bottom of the exit ramp he looked left and then right trying to decide which way to go. To the right the road went on into the countryside and disappeared up a long hill. To the left was a series of shops and a combination truck stop/restaurant.

"Left," Rocky spoke softly. "I gotta go."

Jocko turned left, drove ahead fifty yards to the truck stop driveway, then turned right into the parking lot. He followed the service drive to the building and then slowed nearly to a stop. A blue, four-door, State Police car was parked near the door by the gas pumps, driver's door ajar, engine running. Jocko spun the wheel and drove behind the building to the diesel pumps. He parked at the curb and he and Rocky exited the car. They walked in the rear door of the building, reserved for truck drivers. Rocky disappeared into the men's room and Jocko walked toward the main lobby.

The State Policeman, a young, but large

man, was talking to the clerk. "Bank fraud in Ann Arbor," he was saying. "We have pictures of two of the three suspects. Looks like they swapped cars out on Jackson Road. We believe they're driving a blue or darker color Chevy Impala. A new one." He handed a sheet to the clerk that showed two black and white pictures of Jocko and Rocky wearing their disguises in the bank.

Jocko pretended to look through the racks of candy bars and packages of chips. When the trooper left, Jocko selected a Milky Way Bar and walked to the counter. Rocky joined him carrying two fountain drinks.

"Dr. Pepper?" Jocko asked.

Rocky nodded. Jocko grabbed another candy bar from the rack. A Payday, which he knew was Rocky's favorite. Glancing up, to his alarm, he saw the security monitor. It was rotating pictures from the cameras

49

strategically placed about the business. When the view of the truck pumps flashed on, there was the back fender and part of the trunk of the Impala. Jocko kept his cool, and paid for the snacks. Nodding and smiling to the clerk, he and Rocky left by the truckers' entrance.

A semi was just pulling up to the pumps, forcing the two to walk around the trailer to their car. Jocko glanced around nervously. Nothing seemed out of the ordinary, so he hit the key fob to unlock the doors, and they got in.

"We're not going back on the freeway right away," he thought aloud. The State Police car had just gone under the freeway. As the pair watched, it disappeared under the bridge, then popped up again at the top of the entrance ramp on the far side, gaining speed as the officer merged with the west-bound traffic.

"What'll we do?" Rocky asked.

"It'll be dark soon," Jocko replied. "We'll find a place off the beaten path to stash the loot, then come back in the morning and pick it up. The cops will be looking for us in other places by then. There's a motel back toward town," he said, "just down the road from the truck stop here. We'll lay low for the night, then retrieve the goods tomorrow. It should be smooth sailing into Battle Creek, and we'll meet up with Slim," he concluded.

Chapter Seven

Discovery in the Woods

The children crept closer to the sound of the voices and the twinkling lights. Following the winding path, they kept low and silent, afraid to give their position away. Evy held tight to Candy's collar. multi-floral rose seemed to be everywhere along the trail.   The children hid behind one large bush and peered out.   Two men were standing in a clearing up ahead.   They seemed to be arguing.   They each held a flashlight in his hand.   The larger man spoke in gruff tones.

The three cousins caught snatches of their conversation as they crouched behind the thicket.

"Shoulda' brought some paper and a pen," groused the larger of the two.

"Jeez, Jocko," replied the second, "how'd I know we was gonna' hide the loot? We shoulda' been in Battle Creek by now."

"Okay, okay," replied the guy named Jocko. "I hope you remember exactly where we stashed it, though. It's going to be hard to find when we come back." His tone wasn't so rough now. He placed his hand on the smaller man's shoulder. "Come on now, Rocky, let's go back to the room and call Slim. Then we'll get some sleep."

"If the cops give us a break," whined Rocky. "I can't help thinking they know something. They're everywhere."

"We'll stay in the motel a couple days if

we have to," answered Jocko, "but, if things look clear in the morning, we'll come back and get the loot and take off. It's as easy as that." He took a few steps away, shining his light ahead of him. Rocky started to follow.

Candy, the farm dog, shifted at the men's movement and let out a low growl. Evy took a step to brace herself while restraining Candy, and a twig popped underfoot.

Rocky stopped suddenly and whirled in his tracks, training his light in the children's direction.

"Who's out there?" he demanded nervously. "I heard you."

The children quivered in fear. Evy placed a hand around Candy's muzzle.

Jocko called to Rocky, "Could be anything. It is the middle of the night you know. Maybe a raccoon, deer, or just a stick falling," he said. "No one has had their head bit off by a monster around these parts in over one hundred years. Now come on." With that he turned and picked his way back through the trees and brush.

Rocky stood and directed his light in the children's direction for a moment more and peered into the gloom. Then turning, he gave one last quick glance over his shoulder and hurried after Jocko.

When Rocky's back disappeared into the inky blackness, the children left their hiding place and hustled in the opposite direction, toward the farmstead.

"What were those men doing back there?" Sami asked no one in particular. "They sure sounded mean."

"They were up to no good," Evy said matter-of-factly. "This is Grandma's and Grandpa's farm. Those guys don't belong here." She stopped and shined her light toward Sami and Eli who followed closely behind.

"Maybe we'd better tell Grandpa," Sami responded. Her flashlight showed a nod of agreement from Eli.

Evy glanced nervously over her shoulder, into the darkness, and started walking again.

"We can't say a word," she said. "Grandpa said not to go running around the place at night if we camped in the motor home."

"Especially back in the woods," reminded Sami with emphasis.

"He'd never let us camp out again," complained Eli's voice from behind the girls.

"Then it's settled," Evy declared. "Let's go on back and go to bed. We have chores in the morning," She paused to pat Candy on the head, then set off again.

Chapter Eight

Morning Chores

Eli shoved his plate away and stood up from the table. "That was good, Grandma," he stated enthusiastically. He wiped his mouth on a paper napkin, then said, "French cowboy toast is my favorite." He finished his milk and placed the glass and his plate and silverware on the counter next to the sink. Sami and Evy were still working on their second portion of french toast, fixed Grandma's special way. Eli washed his hands in the back room and went to the door to put on his farm boots. His sister and cousin soon joined him in slipping on their work boots, too.

"Grandpa is out doing chores," their grandma called from the kitchen as the children went out the door. Sami paused to make sure it had latched behind her.

"Okay," she called back to her grandmother.

The children found their grandfather in the chicken coop. He had already raised the small sliding door to the chicken yard, filled the water dispenser, and, with the side of his rubber boot, was stirring the pine shavings used as floor litter. Eli went in the low, wire-covered door to "lend a foot," as he liked to say. Evy picked up the wire egg basket from the other room and stepped through the door to the chicken room. Sami followed closely, pulling the door shut behind her. The nesting room smelled faintly of pine shavings and dry chicken poop. The last of the hens, a reddish-brown one, scurried into the chicken yard through the little door to the west. Evy and Sami began checking for eggs in the soft hay of the metal nesting boxes.

"Got two here," Sami called. She held up a pair of large brown eggs for all to see.

Evy, being the tallest of the three, peered into the top rows of nests. "Got two here, and another here," she exclaimed excitedly. She reached in and produced three more brown eggs and placed them in the wire basket she carried.

Eli stepped over and placed one more egg in. Grandpa checked the nest boxes on the far wall. "Six so far this morning. We can check again this afternoon," he said.

"I'll take them to Grandma," Evy said as she carefully stepped through the low, wire-covered door into the other room, and then out the outside door.

"Meet us in the calf barn," their grandfather called after her. Sami hustled to catch up to her older cousin as Eli and Grandpa walked around the house and down the gravel drive to the red pole building that they all called the calf barn. Puff, the cat, appeared from the lilacs and trailed along behind.

Eli slid open the large door and, stepping inside, flipped on the lights. Two pens, each holding two Holstein spring calves, were in the southeast corner. The calves stood and stretched, tails twitching in greeting. Sami and Evy came through the door all out of breath. They had run from the house. Evy helped Eli slide open the south door. Early morning sunlight streamed in.

"We'll turn them into the barnyard today," Grandpa said, nodding toward the frisky calves. "In a week or so we'll turn them into the regular pasture." He lifted the lid on the grain bin and, grabbing up the scoop, proceeded to fill a gallon pail almost full. He handed it to Sami who lugged it over to the calf pen and, with Grandpa's help, dumped the contents over the boards and into the feeder.

Eli climbed up and over, into the pen, and Evy handed him a six-tined manure fork. She parked a wheelbarrow at the outside edge of the pen. Eli shoved a calf aside with his hip and started cleaning. The deep straw rustled as the calves scampered about while Eli worked around them.

Grandpa picked up a plastic bucket containing a hammer, fence pliers, staples and other fence supplies. "I'll work on that gate latch by the barn," he nodded toward the barnyard. "You kids can finish up and give me a yell when you're done," he added.

"Okay, Grandpa," Sami replied.

Eli stirred the straw with the fork tines as Grandpa walked out through the slider door. As soon as he was gone, Sami whispered, "We should tell Grandpa about the men in the woods last night."

Evy looked at her. Eli flung a blob of manure and straw over the side of the pen and into the wheelbarrow. He put the tines into the straw, leaned on the handle, and looked at Sami.

"It was the middle of the night. At least one o'clock," Eli said. "You know Grandma and Grandpa don't want us in the woods at night unless they're with us."

"Don't you want to camp out ever again?" questioned Evy. "And it was twelve fifty-eight, Eli," Evy glanced at him.

"They were up to no good," Sami replied. "They lost something. Or maybe hid something," she added. "They could be dangerous."

"Don't be a baby," Evy said. "We can always go back later today and look around if you want."

"I don't know," replied Sami doubtfully. To her this sounded like something they would get caught up in and it wouldn't turn out quite right.

"Let's go as soon as we're done here," Eli suggested. "We can check the fences while we're at it." Leaning over the pen, he placed the manure fork over, and climbed out.

Evy strained at the handles of the wheelbarrow and leaned into it to get it moving. She ran the load out the barn door to the corner of the barn lot and, with a heave, dumped it into a small pile.

Eli leaned the manure fork against the barn wall and walked out to find Grandpa. Sami trailed behind, still mulling over in her mind what they had seen and heard last night, and what it could all mean.

Evy parked the wheelbarrow to the side of the barn and hurried to catch up. Grandpa was just finishing the repair on the gate latch. He looked up and smiled as they arrived. "All done?" he questioned.

Eli nodded.

"Me,too," Grandpa said with a nod.

"We thought we'd go for a walk and check fences," Eli told him.

"Yeah," Sami added, "we can count the cows, too."

"Sure. Go ahead," Grandpa said. "The red heifer is due to calf any day now. See if you can find her. If she's in the brush, leave her be as she's probably about to deliver and she'll be feeling cross."

"Okay," replied Evy with a look at Eli and Sami. "We'll let you know."

The three walked out of the barnyard, heading south while their grandfather walked off to another chore.

Sami wandered off the path. "What are you doing?" Eli asked.

"Checking the fence," replied Sami.

"Come on," Evy added. "We can do that on the way back, but do keep your eyes peeled for cattle and new calves."

As the three cousins walked single file into the woods following the cow path, Candy, the farm dog, came up from behind and crowded her way past and to the front of the line. She held her tail high as her nose worked the air.

"Look," Sami pointed left, through the

woods, to the pasture hill beyond. Some cows were grazing contentedly. One reached up to strip some leaves from a small twig overhead.

Eli stopped and peered through the trees. "I count five," he said.

"Look to the right," Evy pointed the way. Three more cows were laying down, chewing their cuds contentedly in the morning sun. Two calves lay together in front of them. "I don't see the red heifer," Evy said.

The trio walked across the wood lot to where the pasture clearing started its ascent up the hill. Candy bounded on ahead and circled the cattle to stand behind them as the children approached.

Eli circled the cows as the calves stretched and sidled closer to their mothers. Then he and Candy walked to the crest of the hill and stopped to peer down to the other side. "She's in a thicket," Eli called to the others. "I don't see a calf yet, but she'll probably have one pretty soon. We'll have to bring Grandpa back later."

He rejoined the others and they continued to the back fence. Candy scooted under the barbed wire while Eli held the top strand for the girls to angle through. They continued on through the woods to a slight thinning where multi-floral rose had established itself. The back woods was dotted with ancient tree stumps from a decades-old logging operation. Here was the spot were they'd heard the voices and saw the lights the night before. Walking on past the clump where they had hidden to eavesdrop on the men, the trio followed Candy as she led them toward the road that ran along the south boundary of the farm. On the other side of the small clearing, they stopped to look around.

"Somebody has been back here," Sami

pointed to crushed grass and some bent limbs on bushes.

Candy sniffed around, nose to the ground, while Evy and Eli followed Sami's lead and began to investigate cautiously, not wanting to disturb any evidence.

"Oh my gosh!" Evy exclaimed. "Look at Candy." The others followed her gaze. The border collie appeared through some brushy overgrowth, carrying a black, baseball-style cap in her teeth.

The children called her over. Eli retrieved the cap from the dog's mouth as she sat expectantly, tail swishing in the leaves and grass. Each child patted and exclaimed over her for her find.

"Maybe it's Grandpa's," Sami said. "He could have lost it."

"He doesn't have a Detroit Tigers hat," Eli replied, somewhat perturbed.

"He'd have mentioned to look for it," Evy added. "You know how cheap he is. Can't stand to lose anything or buy anything new if he can help it. And this hat is almost new," she said.

Eli had handed her the hat and she pointed to the clean straight brim and the inside sweat band.

"He wears only tractor hats or maybe Spring Arbor University, anyway," Eli stated. "He'd say this hat is a goofy hat."

"Who could have left it here?" queried Sami.

"You mean, who lost it," corrected Evy. "Probably the same person who trampled the weeds, and who was back here last night."

"This is a real clue," put in Eli. "Good girl, Candy." They all patted the dog again. She seemed to be proud of her discovery.

"Let's keep looking then," Sami suggested.

"Candy can lead the way."

"Better spread out," Evy stated. "We can follow where someone walked through the grass and weeds."

Sami cautioned, "Watch out for poison ivy."

Following the path made in the grass, the children came to a trampled spot. "Look!" Eli exclaimed. "Somebody stood around here and really mashed the weeds down."

The girls hurried over. Candy sniffed eagerly at the spot and looked toward the road, now only a dozen or so yards away.

"Another clue," Sami had her turn at a discovery. She bent over and picked up a piece of colorful paper.

"Looks like a candy bar wrapper," Evy observed. "A Payday!"

"And look here," Eli pointed to the ground at the edge of where they stood. "A cigarette butt." He picked it up and held it gingerly between his thumb and forefinger, all the while making a face of disgust.

"That's littering. And smoking isn't good for you," Sami stated emphatically.

"But they're clues," Evy said. "Someone was back here alright. They stood around, maybe talking."

"Maybe they were looking for this hat," Sami offered.

"Maybe they were doing something else and lost the hat back here in the dark," Evy countered. "We know we saw two lights, two men, and heard two voices. What were they up to?"

"No good, that's for sure," replied Eli not wanting to be left out of the discussion. "Grandpa never mentioned any of his friends setting up hunting blinds or deer stands. He'd be sure to mention it if they were."

71

"Nobody sets up a deer blind in the middle of the night or at this time of the year," Evy reminded him.

Her cousins nodded in agreement. The three turned to follow the trail through the trees and through the tall grass toward the road. They stopped abruptly at the ditch that paralleled the road. "Should we jump it?" Sami asked while surveying the width of the depression.

Eli said, "It's not too wide."

"We should ride our bikes around the block and look for clues on the road," Evy suggested. She nodded toward the far side of the ditch where a path could plainly be seen through the high grass.

"We do need to get back," Eli stated. Grandma and Grandpa will wonder where we are, and what happened to us."

The girls nodded in agreement and turned

to start back to the house. "We can check fences and the red heifer on the way back," Evy said, "and we'd better hide these clues for now. Don't want to get Grandma and Grandpa all stirred up."

The children returned to the house, checking fences, and stopping to observe the red heifer and a wobbly new calf.

At the red pole barn, Evy stuck the hat, now containing the other clues, up into the straw loft over the calf pens. The trio went to the house to report on the new calf.

Chapter Nine

News of the Crime

The children reported to their grandfather and then walked with him to the back pasture to check out the new calf. It turned out to be a bull. Grandpa was happy with its progress, so they left the red heifer alone with her new calf and returned to the house.

To pass the rest of the morning, the cousins played dominoes with their grand-parents. After lunch they helped stack a pickup load of firewood. As the afternoon warmed up, Grandpa walked with the children up the lane to the mail box. Upon their return, he selected a shady spot in the front yard to relax.

The children settled at a picnic table where they began playing a good-natured, but boisterous, card game of Uno. Grandma brought out a tray of glasses filled with icy lemonade. They all sat enjoying their drinks as Grandpa browsed through the newspaper. He stopped short and began reading.

"Listen to this," he said. "Yesterday afternoon there was a robbery at a bank in Ann Arbor. 'The main branch of the Citizens' Trust Bank was robbed when two men wearing disguises impersonated customers in the safety deposit box department.'" he read. "'The deposit box contained jewels, rare coins, stock certificates, and a large amount of cash.'"

He looked up before continuing. "It says here that the two robbers didn't show any weapons or threaten anyone, just signed the registry and presented fake I.D. 'Witnesses said the men escaped in a silver Toyota sedan,'" he quoted the paper. "'The car was later found abandoned on the back lot of a car dealership off west Jackson Road.' Well," said Grandpa, "Says here that the gang swapped the get-a-way car for a blue, or darker color, four-door sedan. And, they were last seen on I-94 west-bound."

"The police think there were three men, but a fuel station camera at Exit 130 shows two of the suspects getting into the car. Those are the last clues the police have," Grandpa said.

The children stopped their card game and looked at him.

He read some more, then looked up, "The

trail ends west of Jackson. Hmm, that would put them right in our area. Imagine that. A bank heist and the bad guys end up out here. That would add some excitement to our summer, wouldn't it? I wonder if there will be a reward offered?" Grandpa's face lit up.

The cousins glanced knowingly at each other.

"May I read that when you're done," Evy asked her grandfather.

"Sure, take it now. I'll read the sports," he replied while handing over the front section of the paper.

"Come on guys," Evy called to the others. She took the paper and walked around the house and up the driveway to the hay barn, leaving the others to catch up. The cousins followed Evy up the ladder to the mow and into the hay fort that their grandfather had helped them build. They settled in, backs against the bales, Evy on one side, Eli and Sami facing her from the other. Evy drew her knees up and laid the newspaper across her legs. "Listen," she said, as she began reading aloud. "It says the men are thought to have worn disguises and ditched them after the robbery."

"I like heist better," said Eli.

Evy and Sami gave him a sharp look and Evy continued, "Police thought they had the car spotted on west-bound I-94 in eastern Jackson County. They're asking any citizens with information to contact Detective Bennett of the Ann Arbor Police Department, or the local authorities."

"Were they wearing a Detroit Tigers hat?" queried Sami.

"It doesn't say," replied Evy. "But why would bank robbers be in Grandpa's woods? To hide the loot they stole?" She asked the questions the others were thinking.

"We didn't see anything," Sami put in, "and if we find jewels, do we get to keep them?"

"Do we get to keep the money?" Eli asked brightly.

"There are no jewels or money hidden back there," Evy replied, disgustedly. "And, if there were, we couldn't keep it. That would be dishonest."

"Finders keepers," Eli said with a broad grin.

"Maybe there's a tiara," Sami interjected hopefully.

"Yeah, and maybe they they left a rainbow unicorn to guard the treasure," Evy replied with a hint of sarcasm.

Sami's eyes lit up at the thought of it.

"What else does it say?" Eli wanted to know.

"Here," Evy said, handing over the paper.

"There's not much more. But, first thing tomorrow, maybe we should ride our bikes around the block and look for more clues."

"I'll take my Cub Cadet," Eli's face brightened.

"Our bicycles," Evy replied firmly. "Grandpa won't let you drive a lawn mower on the road. Not even out here."

Eli looked crestfallen. He loved to drive his classic Cub Cadet that he and Grandpa had worked on. With Sami looking over his shoulder, he continued to scan the newspaper article. "It says here that there were three suspects in Ann Arbor, but only two were spotted on the security tape at the fuel station west of Jackson. I wonder what happened to the third guy?"

"Maybe the guys on the tape weren't the suspects," Sami concluded.

"Or they dropped him off somewhere," Evy

added.

Her cousins looked at her questioningly. "But for what reason?" Eli asked.

Evy shrugged. "They had a falling out, or possibly the third guy wasn't all that involved," she said.

"Or, maybe he didn't want to be a bad guy," Sami offered.

"Let's get our bikes and look for more clues," Evy suggested. "Maybe those we found aren't connected to the heist, but if they are, we need to report it to the police. And if we have some more clues, all the better."

"I think we need to tell Grandpa first," Sami added. "He'll know what to do."

"When we have some solid proof," Evy replied, "and remember, we're not supposed to be wandering around the farm at night unless an adult is with us."

"Especially back in the woods," added

Sami, crossing her arms and nodding for emphasis.

Eli folded the paper. The children climbed from the mow and walked to the pole barn to check on their bicycles. Grandpa helped oil the chains and adjust the seats as they told of their plan to ride around the block, not mentioning the search at the back of the farm.

"Be careful. Watch for traffic," he reminded them.

Chapter Ten

An Unwelcome Stranger

After morning chores, the children rode
their bicycles around the country square to
the gravel road that skirted the south side of
the farm. Candy, the farm dog, accompanied
them, trotting alongside.

"Here's the place," Evy stopped her bike.
Eli and Sami braked to a stop beside her,
their tires crunching on the small stones.

"More cigarette butts," Sami said in disgust.

"Looks like somebody stood around for a while here, too," Evy pointed out. "See the gravel." She nodded to two sets of footprints and packed gravel and dirt at the shoulder of the road.

"There's where they came across the ditch," pointed out Eli, "and the car spun its tires when it left." He knelt beside a shallow trough in the gravel with scattered stones behind it.

Sami dropped her bike in the grass at the edge of the road. Eli and Evy followed her actions and walked the path through the tall weeds to the ditch. Candy, the farm dog, forced her way through the vegetation and into the lead.

A car's tires could be heard turning the corner from the paved road onto the gravel.

The children stopped to look back as a dark blue, four-door sedan slowed. Two men were in the front seat. The driver had a rough face and dark hair. The other was of slighter build and had lighter hair. They stared at the children as the car crept past at low speed.

"What was that about?" Eli wondered aloud.

"Oh my gosh!" Evy exclaimed. "Two men in a dark blue four-door. That's what the paper said."

"There are a lot of blue cars," Eli replied. "They could have been driving by and wondered what we were doing back here. That's why they slowed down. Though it sure is a coincidence," he added thoughtfully.

"I say we follow the path and go look for hidden treasure," Sami said.

Candy bounded ahead, as the children following closely behind. The three cousins leaped across the ditch and into the tall grass. A path where the grass and weeds were knocked down was plainly evident. Following the trail into the woods, the three discovered the dimness beneath the trees soon obscured the way.

"Where to now?" queried Sami peering around in the gloom. It took a moment for the children's eyes to adjust to the reduced light of the woods.

"Here!" Eli called. He and Candy had run ahead. "See the clump of weeds here and the branch." Some low plants were trampled and a broken branch showed the way.

Dodging clumps of grasping multi-floral rose, the trio soon found themselves standing in the small clearing where they had found clues the previous morning.

"If you were hiding stolen property, where would you put it back here?" Evy stood with hr hands on her hips and looked around.

"Under a rock?" asked Sami. "Or up a tree?"

Eli looked up. "Maybe in a squirrels nest!"

Sami started scanning the trees with him.

"Who in their right mind would climb into a tree top in the middle of the night?" Evy asked them. "But a tree might be the answer. Suppose a bag or small box were hidden in a hollow tree or in a crotch where large limbs come together," she speculated.

Eli wandered to some trees at the side of the clearing and began to circle them, searching the ground and the trunks. Suddenly Candy growled softly and, grabbing his shirt sleeve in her teeth, attempted to pull him back to the others.

"You're not much help, Candy," Eli told her. "What's gotten into you?"

Candy responded by dropping his sleeve and

87

barking at the woods in the direction from which the children came. She growled deep in her throat and took a few steps toward the woods.

"Call off your dog," a man's voice startled them. "I'm not dangerous, honest," he added.

"Bad doggie," Sami shook her finger at Candy.

Evy clapped her hands and called Candy to her side. Holding the dog's collar, she asked, "Can we help you with something?"

"Not really," the stranger answered pleasantly. He was of medium height with dark hair and a solid build. He wore blue jeans and running shoes with a light-colored golf shirt. "I'm just exploring the countryside," he explained. "I work for a company that buys land in the country."

"This is my grandparent's farm," Evy

responded. "It's not for sale." She recognized the man as the driver of the blue sedan that they had just seen on the road, and became suspicious of his motives.

"We're going to inherit the farm," Eli stated firmly.

"Well, I guess I'll be going then," was the man's reply.

He glanced about in the woods in a way that made Evy doubt his story. She still held firmly to Candy's collar. The dog kept growling low in her throat and Evy didn't bother to quiet her.

Turning to walk out of the woods, the stranger seemed to take his time. Evy tightened her grip on Candy's collar as the children followed at a distance.

"Those must be your bicycles," the man called to them over his shoulder. "They look like fun."

"Yes," replied Sami. "We ride them a lot when we're visiting."

Evy glanced at Sami with a look that told her to keep quiet. Candy still let the occasional rumble escape her throat.

At the roadside, the man stopped. Candy immediately stopped some distance back and turned to block the path so the children couldn't proceed. She pressed against Evy's legs.

Noticing the dog's defensive posture, the man stepped across the ditch to the road. The dog allowed the children to proceed to their bikes.

Another stranger, who Evy recognized as the car's passenger, waited a little way down the road, leaning against the rear fender of the blue sedan. He took one last puff on a cigarette and dropped the still smoldering butt into the gravel. He smiled at the

children but said nothing. The man from the
woods took a few steps toward the car, then
stopped and turned to watch as the three
cousins picked up their bikes. Candy stood
between the three cousins and the strangers.

"Have a good day," the stranger called.

"It's not for sale," Eli replied looking
back as he shoved hard on his pedals to catch
up with Sami and Evy.

Candy gave one last growl and turned to
trot alongside Eli.

The man stood smiling and watched them
leave, then turned and walked back to the car.
"I didn't see your hat back there," he said to
Rocky. "You're lucky you don't lose your
head, too. You would if it wasn't screwed on
tight," he groused.

"It was practically brand new," Rocky
looked dejected.

The men got into the car.

Chapter Eleven

Discovered!

During a lunch of ham sandwiches, french fries, fruit, and milk, together at the picnic table in the shade of the front yard, the cousins talked about what it all could mean.

Eli said, "Something is hidden in the woods and we can't find it."

"Some *thing* is hidden in the woods and *they* can't find it," Evy emphasized the words "thing and they."

"Could there be jewels and a crown?" asked Sami before diving into another sandwich wedge.

Eli took a sip of his lemonade and looked thoughtful. "I think they put their treasure in a hole in the ground or maybe in a rotten stump or tree trunk."

Evy was quiet for a moment and stared off into space, lost in her own thoughts. She turned to Eli, "What was the guy doing by the car?" she questioned.

"He was smoking," Eli and Sami answered at the same time.

"Right," Evy replied, "and what clue did we find in the clearing yesterday? And on the gravel at the roadside this morning?"

"A cigarette butt," Eli answered. Then his face brightened. "I see where you're going with this. The guy threw his cigarette down. If it's the same brand as what we found, then they definitely are the two who were back in the woods the other night."

"And they're up to no good," reminded Sami, with a nod of her head.

"We need to walk back through the woods and investigate the side of the road where the car was parked," Evy said.

Her cousins nodded in agreement, and leaned closer to whisper their plans.

After evening chores the cousins walked back along the cow path and came to the barbed wire fence that divided the wood lot.

Slipping through the wire, Candy, the farm dog, stopped and growled low in her throat. Her ears pricked up and her nose worked the air.

Evy reached for her collar to restrain her.

"Let her go," Eli told Evy. "Let her see

what's in the woods." He stepped forward with the dog and, as before, Candy blocked the path.

In the distance, a car door slammed. It was then that the sound of voices reached the children's ears. Now it was Eli's turn to grab Candy's collar and quiet her with soothing sounds. The children crept cautiously ahead.

"I knew we should have written down where we put the loot," Jocko's harsh voice echoed through the trees.

"It's got to be right in this area," Rocky's voice replied. "I put it in one of these old stumps, but it's hard to tell which one, seeing as how it was pitch black out here." His voice sounded a little uncertain.

"Well, Slim's gonna wonder what we did with it," Jocko replied. "He's getting concerned, you know. But I can handle him.

Now, let's just try this search again. We'll
start in the clearing and work in wider
circles. The loot's got to be here."

"Unless those pesky kids found it," Rocky
offered.

At Rocky's words, the three cousins looked
at each other wide eyed with the realization
that they were the "pesky kids!" They
crouched lower behind another clump of multi-
floral rose.

Evy put her mouth close to Eli's ear,
"What exactly are the men looking for?" she
whispered. Eli's and Sami's faces asked the
same thing.

Jocko said, "They would have blabbed to
the police if they'd found it. They're not
around to interfere now, so let's get
started." He walked to a nearby stump and
peered around it. "Nope," he replied.

Rocky started at the other side of the

clearing and began his search.

As he neared the area where the cousins were concealed, a low growl escaped Candy's throat.

Rocky nearly fell over himself in his surprise. "Who's there?" he shouted nervously into the gathering gloom.

"What's the matter now?" Jocko demanded from the other side of the clearing. "You trying to get the whole neighborhood back here?" He didn't sound very happy.

"I think they're already here," was Rocky's reply.

Candy slipped from Eli's grasp and stepped out onto the path.

"It's just a dog," Rocky nervously assured Jocko.

"The same dog that was with those kids this morning, you fool," Jocko said.

Evy tapped Eli and Sami on their shoulders

and turned, still crouching, and began working her way back the way they came.

Rocky spotted them. "It's those darn kids," he called back to Jocko. "I bet they took our loot."

Candy made a feint at him as he stepped forward to give chase. Rocky stopped abruptly and watched as the children stood and ran back into the woods. Candy let go with one more low growl and turned to follow them.

"Let them go," Jocko groused. "I told ya, they don't have it. This place would've been crawling with cops if they had. Now let's get out of here before the cops do show up. We'll come back tonight with some lights. It'll be dark in another hour or so and those kids will be in bed." He turned to walk back to the road and to the car. He paused to check a few stumps and rotten logs on the way.

Rocky turned to follow, checking the same

stumps that Jocko had checked. He shook his head dejectedly.

"It's got to be here," he muttered to himself. "Got to be here."

Chapter Twelve

Plan for Another Search

The children hurried back through the woods. Once back in the pasture, and away from the dark woods, the children relaxed. Candy had ceased her low growling and her hackles lay smooth.

"We should go back tonight and find the treasure," Eli finally spoke.

"Not on your life," put in Sami. "You

heard that guy, he thinks we already have it."
She shrugged, "Whatever *it* is. Boy, they both
sounded pretty mean to me. Especially that
one guy."

"The one called Jocko?" Evy asked. "He's
scary." And she trembled at the thought of
him.

"We can still go back later and look
around," said Eli. "Candy will be with us if
there's trouble. We don't need to find any
more cigarette butts. Those are the guys
alright," he added firmly.

"We only have 'til Sunday before we
leave," Evy replied. "Today is Wednesday, so
we have tonight and two days to find the
hidden stuff and report to the police."

"What exactly are we looking for?"
questioned Eli. "A box? Maybe a bag? And
how big is it?"

"Whatever is hidden can't be too big,"

replied Evy. "It has to fit in a hollow tree stump, remember?"

"We were on the right track before, when we were looking in stumps and hollow trees," Eli said.

Sami had been silent throughout the conversation. "I don't like this at all," she finally said. "Especially that mean guy. He scares me. We need to tell Grandpa. He'll know what to do."

"He'll think we made the whole thing up," replied Evy. "However, we do have the evidence we found the other day, and if we can find some more clues and even the loot, we have a case."

"There are a lot of stumps and dead trees back there," Sami said, with a nod of agreement from Eli.

"We know the general area," replied Evy thoughtfully, "and if we start our search in the clearing, we're bound to come across the hiding place."

"We should take Candy with us and go back tonight when nobody will be around," Eli offered.

"Just what I was thinking," replied Evy.

"I think we should tell Grandpa," Sami reminded them.

"We will," Evy reassured her. "Let's just give it a good search, then we'll tell Grandpa even if we don't find the loot. I'm convinced this has something to do with the bank heist we read about in the paper. The article is still stashed up in the hay loft, where we moved the clues that we found. We'll gather it all up and show Grandpa tomorrow morning," she concluded.

Her cousins agreed, though Sami reluctantly so. Eli opened the gate at the red barn and the children went through.

Chapter Thirteen

Another Search

The blue Impala stopped in front of a room at a nearby, one-story motel, just south of the I-94 intersection. Jocko shifted the gear selector into park, then turned to Rocky. "If you'd remember where you put things we wouldn't have this problem." He shook his head in disgust.

"Me?" Rocky exclaimed. "You were there, too, you know. And what are we gonna do about those kids?" The temperature was climbing and Rocky wiped his brow with a paper napkin from a fast food restaurant.

Jocko said, "Those kids won't be back for a while. That is, unless they go blab to the authorities. If they do show up again, I'll take care of them, and that dog, too," he muttered threateningly.

"I think we need to go deeper into the woods," Rocky suggested. "I remember the stump being big around. And it's hollow, like a kettle. There was a hollow between the roots, too. That's where I shoved the stuff. You saw me."

Rocky snarled, "I had other things on my mind. Like if the cops were tailing us. I can't watch every move you make." He shook his head disgustedly. "Do I have to do everything around here?"

Rocky was silent for a moment. "I'm just

sayin' we both were there and we both can find it. I think we're not going far enough back in the woods," he said. "We wanted to get off the beaten path and that's where we went. Let's go back tonight and walk in deeper. Those darn kids will be in bed. Nobody will bother us and we can take our time," he concluded.

Jocko smiled. "I can go along with that. No need to get excited yet. You're right about no one being out in the middle of the night. We'll have hours to search if we need it. Let's go get a bite to eat, and then some sleep." He started the car and pulled onto the roadway. "Yeah," he said aloud, "the middle of the night ought to do it."

Chapter Fourteen

Perplexed Detective

Detective Bennett turned his coffee cup slowly in his hands then let it settle to his desk, the heavy ceramic thudding as it made contact. He turned the blue U of M logo to face him, then picked up a well-worn pencil. For the tenth time, he looked over the yellow legal pad that lay to the right of the half-empty cup of cold coffee. Something was

bugging him about the bank job at Citizens'
Trust. He went down his list again, looking
for something that the bad guys had forgotten.
There was always something, it seemed, that
tripped them up. It was his experience that
most criminals weren't exactly geniuses, even
though they thought they were. There was
always some little detail that would give them
away. He just had to find it. He re-read his
list:

Two men with fake I.D.s - probably wearing
disguises, signed out a deposit box and got
away with vintage jewelry, coins, some cash,
and securities.

One of the men was probably the one who
worked for a private citizen as a handyman and
is suspected of robbing the safe in his
employer's study. Papers obtained in the
first robbery yielded signatures and
identification for the crooks to bluff their

way into the bank.

A college student I.D.'d the suspects and their getaway car, a silver Toyota four-door sedan. The sedan was later recovered on the back lot of a car dealer out on West Jackson Road. No prints were lifted from the car. A partial print was lifted from the key set that an officer had discovered in the brush at the edge of the lot.

Two male juveniles had reported three men leaving the Toyota and taking a dark blue, four-door Chevrolet Impala. They gave a description of the men that was different from the one given by the bank employees and the college student. This reinforced Bennett's belief that the men wore disguises during the bank job.

"Good disguises, too," the detective thought out loud. He made a mental note to see if there was any evidence the men had access to theatrical props.

"You say something?" a head peered around his office door.

"Good to see you, Smitty. Just tossing out ideas is all," Bennett replied. "Have a seat a minute and let me bounce some stuff off you."

Smitty sat in the chair by the door. He took a sip of the fresh coffee he had just gotten from the machine on the table down the hall from Bennett's office. "What ya' got?" he asked.

Bennett went over the list again and added a few more ideas. "We thought the Impala was headed west on I-94," he concluded. "We lost it in the Jackson area. Could have gone north, or for that matter, south on U.S. 27," he mused. "By now the bad guys could have ditched it for yet another car," he said.

At that moment a large body appeared in

the office doorway. "Got something for you, Bennett," a mountain of a man in a crumpled brown suit announced. "State boys in Jackson sent it over. Check your e-mail." He nodded toward the computer on Bennett's desk.

Smitty stood up, smiled at the large man, and stepped to Bennett's desk to peer over his shoulder at the monitor. Bennett clicked on an icon and his e-mail account opened up. Unopened and saved e-mails filled the page. He ran the cursor up and down the screen a few times and found the message he wanted. Clicking it open, he leaned back in his chair and waited. A brief message appeared from the State Police post in Jackson with an attachment. Bennett clicked on it. A grainy black and white tape showed the back portion of a dark-colored, newer model Chevy Impala. It was clearly at a service station, as semis drove past, obscuring the picture for a moment, then were gone.

"Where's that from?" Smitty questioned from over Bennett's shoulder. He turned to the door to ask the big guy, but the big guy had already gone.

"Says here from Exit 130, west of Jackson," the detective replied. "I'll get a hold of the State guys and get some more info," he continued. "I might just be taking a trip tomorrow morning."

"Good luck with that," Smitty said, clapping a hand on Bennett's shoulder. "Who knows what might turn up if you kick over enough stones."

"I could use some company, you know," Bennett looked at him through tired eyes.

"See what I can do," Smitty replied as he checked his watch and walked out the door. Bennett returned to the e-mail to see what he'd missed. Clicking the respond button, he began typing a letter of inquiry to the State Police post in Jackson. He checked the time in the lower right-hand corner of the display. Seven-thirty in the evening, long past time to go home. He tidied up his desk a bit and shut down the computer, hoping there would be a positive e-mail from the Jackson post waiting for him in the morning.

At seven A.M. the next morning, the office was just beginning to stir with the arrival of first shift. Bennett, refreshed with a good night's sleep and a hearty breakfast, had been at his desk for half an hour. He'd just finished lining up an unmarked car from the garage when there was a knock on his office door.

"Looks like you've got a partner for the day," Smitty announced joyfully.

"Good," Bennett replied. "I'll need somebody to eat the other half of the pizza."

He smiled over at his friend.

"Mushrooms and ham?" Smitty raised his eyebrows.

"You're on," Bennett replied good naturedly, picking up his brief case. His computer display was shutting down behind him.

Twenty minutes later the detectives were west bound on Jackson Road.

"First stop, a corner gas station two blocks south of Jackson Road," Bennett announced. "Got a phone message this morning from the manager. The manager said the night crew found some stuff in the trash during clean up."

"Oh?" Smitty looked interested.

"Ya, found some clothes and fake beard, mustache, and wigs. This oughta' be good."

"Sounds like our boys," his friend replied with a grin.

They made good progress as most of the

morning traffic was inbound to downtown Ann
Arbor. Bennett swung into the parking lot of
the corner gas station and convenience store.
Putting the shift lever up into park, he used
the key fob to pop open the trunk. He stepped
out of the car and Smitty did the same.
Walking to the open trunk, Bennett lifted the
lid and extracted two pairs of surgical gloves
and a large plastic zip-lock bag. He handed a
pair of gloves to Smitty and put his in his
pocket. Slamming shut the trunk lid, he
walked with his partner to the building. A
friendly, middle-aged man greeted them with a
welcoming smile. Two clerks were behind the
counter cashing out the gas customers at the
self-serve pumps, and ringing up cup after cup
of coffee and breakfast rolls.

"Good morning, gentlemen," the man said.

"Good morning," Bennett returned his
greeting. "Are you Mr. Soules?" he inquired,

extending his hand.

Soules took the detective's hand and shook it warmly. "I am he," he said while glancing at Smitty and then back to Bennett.

"Detectives Bennett and Smith," Bennett produced his badge and identification tag. "We're here about the items found in the trash last night. We really appreciate the call."

Smith nodded his head in agreement.

"Glad to help out, officers," the friendly manager said. "Right this way," he directed them to a room at the back of the building that looked out over the store through a one-way window.

In the room, Soules took a brown paper bag from behind a desk and handed it to Bennett, who had already slipped on his surgical gloves. Smitty did the same.

"Anybody handle the stuff," he said, peering into the bag.

"Just the night guys," replied the manager. "Two of them. They thought something didn't seem right. Then one remembered news reports about the bank heist downtown, so they put everything back in the bag."

Setting the bag on the desk, Bennett removed a brown wig, two shirts, two pairs of khaki pants, a fake mustache, and a beard.

"One guy wore a Van Dyke," he looked at Smitty while holding up the beard in his gloved hand.

"Bingo!" exclaimed his partner.

Bennett grinned and nodded in agreement. Searching through the pockets of the shirts and pants, he found nothing. He began placing the items back in the paper bag, then placed it all into the large, clear, resealable plastic bag. Next, he placed a phone call to headquarters for a patrol unit to come pick up the new evidence for delivery to the lab.

Finally, he and Smitty took a look at the men's room and the trash can. Everything was clean, as Bennett knew it would be. The night crew had done their job well.

A black and white unit soon appeared and Bennett turned the evidence over to the two patrolmen, who promptly left with it for the downtown police lab.

Saying goodbye to the manager, Mr. Soules, Bennett and Smitty resumed their journey west-bound on I-94 to Jackson.

Chapter Fifteen

Captured!

Evy roused Eli and Sami from their blankets where they slept deeply. Much to their grandparents' wonderment, they had gone to bed at first dusk, camping in the motor home.

"It's one o'clock," Evy said, "let's get going."

Eli waved her away with his hand. "Let's

go tomorrow," he said sleepily.

"I'm ready," Sami threw back her blanket and swung her legs over the edge of the bunk.

"I'm coming, too," Eli groused as he slipped his socks and boots on.

Armed with flashlights, the children proceeded back the trail into the murky woods.

Following the now familiar path, the trio soon arrived at the small clearing on the south end of the farm. Candy, the farm dog, moved quietly ahead.

"This is the spot," Evy directed with her light. "If we each take a side we can search in a circle then gradually increase the search into the woods."

Wide awake now, in the cool of the night, Eli and Sami nodded their agreement. Candy followed along with Sami as she directed her light at a tree on the clearing edge.

"Don't forget trees, too," she suggested.

"Whatever we're looking for could even be on the ground hidden by grass or brush," Eli suggested. He shined his light down at his feet and around him.

Evy and Sami did the same as they payed careful attention to the little clearing in the middle of the dark woods. Within minutes their search turned up empty-handed.

"Let's work together working in a circle," Evy suggested. Three pairs of eyes are better than one," she concluded.

"This tree is a good place to start," Eli cast his light at a large, gnarled maple at the edge of the clearing.

"Don't forget the old stumps," Sami added, not wanting to be left out. "There are dozens of them back here."

"Grandpa says the woods was logged several years before he and Grandma bought the farm," Evy said, "and they've been here for over thirty years."

"We learned in school that the whole area was logged off in pioneer days," Eli added as he peered into the hollow of a rotted stump near the large maple. "Trees were a bother back then, and many were dropped, then burned in brush piles to clear the land," he added.

Sami searched the clumps of grass and brush around the stump.

Evy wandered off a few yards to closely examine a fallen log. One end had a hollow crevice. Suddenly she jumped back. "Something is in there!" she exclaimed.

Eli and Sami rushed over, as Candy, the farm dog, sniffed and snuffed at the opening in the log end.

"Is it the treasure?" questioned Sami as she stooped to shine her light along with Eli's into the depths of the log. Candy backed off a step as growling and hissing came from the hollow. The children stepped back also, and a rather angry opossum emerged from the log and scurried away into the woods.

The cousins heaved a sigh of relief. Candy stared at the path the opossum had taken, then turned to poke her snout into the log and sniff and snuff some more. Evy gently pulled her back and then directed her light into the hollow to examine it further.

"I hope it's in there," Sami said.

"Yeah," Eli nodded in agreement, a broad smile on his face.

With the log holding the children's attention, they didn't notice the sounds of the woods surrounding them. Eli picked up one of the many sticks littering the area, and stooped to intently poke into the far reaches of the hollow.

"Nothing," he stood up shaking his head. Letting the stick drop, he guided his light to another area. Evy and Sami hopefully double-checked the cavity before moving on. Candy walked with the girls, obviously enjoying the searching game.

Eli wandered to a large, moldy stump and pointed his flashlight down into the rotted core while the girls searched the brush around an ancient oak. A hollow drew their attention. It was about the level of Sami's face. Candy stood on her hind legs, leaned against the tree, and sniffed expectantly.

Not far away, Eli continued to investigate the area around the old stump. A sudden noise caused him to turn abruptly and aim his light to the other side of the clearing.

"You kids are always interfering," Jocko's harsh voice snarled. He moved quickly toward Eli.

Surprised, Eli took a step backward. Caught off guard, he stumbled against the stump and crashed to the ground, dropping his flashlight!

Jocko lunged at Eli, grabbing him by the shoulder before he could roll out of range.

A few yards away, Evy and Sami gasped as Jocko's muscular arms pinned the squirming Eli to him!

Chapter Sixteen

Decision

"Let go of me!" Eli shouted as he struggled against his capture.

"You kids are poking your noses in where you don't belong!" Jocko snarled. "Rocky," he shouted over his shoulder, "help me get this kid to the car!"

Rocky hesitated. "What about the others?" He directed a glance at the girls who stood nervously a few yards away.

"They'll come along if they know what's good for them." Jocko gave them a hard look. "This one goes in the trunk, then the others will behave. We'll give them a little midnight ride that will keep them busy while we search the woods." He gave a hard laugh.

Eli continued to struggle in vain against Jocko's tight grip. "I'm telling my grandpa," he shouted.

Jocko laughed in response. "It won't do you any good, kid," he sneered.

Upon hearing this, Evy, who had been restraining Candy, released her grip from the dog's collar and yelled, "Get 'im Candy."

The border collie sprang into action. Baring her teeth, she charged at Jocko, who tried to kick her away while still restraining Eli. Candy dodged his foot and whirled to sink her teeth into his calf muscle and held

on. Jocko howled in pain and tried to shake
the dog off.

Evy stooped to pick up a stout limb
and held it high over her shoulder, like a
baseball bat, and stepped forward.

"You're a bad man!" Sami shouted. "I hope
you get a tick! And I hope you pee your
pants, too!" She chucked a stick at Jocko's
head. The man ducked instinctively as the
stick sailed wide.

Evy swung her heavy limb threateningly,
barely missing Jocko's head. Rocky retreated
back several steps, not wanting to tangle with
the dog or Evy with her makeshift club. Jocko
waved his left arm defensively.

Eli continued to struggle, then mimicked
Candy's attack method by biting down hard on
Jocko's right arm that still encircled him.

As the children continued to holler at
Jocko, the big man yelped in pain again, and

released Eli from his grip. Wide-eyed from his close encounter, Eli ran to Evy's side where Sami handed him his flashlight and patted his back sympathetically.

Rocky had already turned to follow the path out of the woods, his light casting an eerie glow on the tree limbs and brush. Candy released her grip on Jocko's leg and backed off, still growling menacingly deep in her throat.

Jocko rubbed his injured arm, then turned his attention to his leg as he hobbled along after Rocky. "You'll pay for this, you little brats!" he declared.

The children turned to retreat the other way on the path through the woods to the cow pasture and on to the barnyard.

"I-I-I'm telling Grandpa," Sami stammered.

"I agree," said Evy, shaken from the encounter. "Those two are sure after something. And I wonder where the third guy is that the paper mentioned." She walked briskly, causing the others to trot along to keep up. "There's something back there that those men want and they can't find it," she added.

Candy, the farm dog, hung back. She turned her head frequently to listen for sounds of someone following through the woods.

"We have to tell Grandpa and Grandma," Eli said with a shudder. He was still trembling from his experience. "They need to call the police."

"It's agreed then," Evy countered, "we'll tell them in the morning.

Chapter Seventeen

Telling Grandpa

The children finished their morning chores in the hen house. As Evy and Sami carried the egg basket to the house, Eli ran to the farm shop where Grandpa was busy.

He found him leaning over the fender of his white Studebaker Daytona four-door. His other Studebaker, the gray two-door hardtop, sat in the next bay, hood up, awaiting its turn.

The fenders and grill-work of the white car were draped with old furniture quilts to protect the paint and give Grandpa a soft cushion to lean on.

He withdrew his head from under the hood, holding the oil dipstick in his right hand. He smile broadly at Eli. For once Eli stood silently. Evy and Sami arrived from the house and appeared in the open doorway.

Eli looked at them expectantly. "Hi, Grandpa," Evy said. "We have a question for you, and maybe something to tell you." She had been rehearsing her talk in her mind and hoped it came out the way she'd practiced it.

"What can I do for you kids this morning?" Grandpa asked. He reached over to where Puff, the cat, sat on the fender, and scratched behind his ear. The cat purred loudly.

"Well," Eli nervously shifted his weight from foot to foot. "Do you remember the article in the paper a few days back about the bank heist in Ann Arbor?"

"Sure do," Grandpa replied as he wiped oil from the dipstick, and turned to replace it in the Studebaker's V/8. He looked at Eli, "Do you need to use the bathroom?"

Eli stopped dancing from foot to foot and stood still. Grandpa turned to face the children again.

"We think the bad guys hid their stolen property on the back of our farm," Sami blurted. "And one of them tried to kidnap Eli!" she fairly shouted.

The children's grandfather raised his eyebrows in surprise. Wiping his hands on an oil rag, he said, "Pull up a chair and tell me all about this." He leaned against the fender of the Studebaker as the children pulled up

133

shop stools and sat down.

Puff stood, stretched, then jumped down from the fender and sauntered out the door.

Evy sat on the roll-around stool with the adjustable height. She produced the newspaper clipping and handed it to her grandfather.

"We think the robbers hid their loot in the woods while trying to get away from the police," Evy said.

"Only now they can't find it," Eli added excitedly.

"Just a minute, kids," Grandpa said. "You must have some kind of proof. And what's this about someone trying to kidnap Eli?"

Evy explained, "We were in the back woods last night searching for the loot, when a man came along and grabbed Eli." So far the conversation wasn't going as she had imagined. Turning to Eli and Sami, she asked them to retrieve the hat and other evidence from the hiding place in the hay fort where the children had moved it.

"Be right back!" they yelled while leaping from their seats and dashing out the open, overhead door. The sounds of their feet on the gravel drive faded as they ran to the hay barn.

Evy turned back to her grandfather. "We heard noises in the woods one night," she said. "Creeping back through the woods, we discovered two men who were arguing about where they had left something. They didn't see us and when they left, we came back to the house."

"How late at night was this?" her grandfather asked. Evy knew where this was going and didn't try to hide the fact that it was the middle of the night.

Just then Eli and Sami returned. They briskly walked in and handed a hat to Grandpa.

"This looks almost new," he said. "Where did you say you found it? In the back woods?"

"Yes," the children replied in unison. "Candy found it, and look what else we found," Sami held out a baggie with several cigarette butts, and a candy bar wrapper in it.

"We found one in the woods where the men were standing, and the others the next day at the side of the road behind the woods," Evy explained.

"Smoking is bad for you," Sami made a face.

Grandpa smiled. "Yes it is," he replied. "Now start at the beginning and tell me everything. Evy, you go first."

Evy told about the walk around the farm during the night with Candy, the farm dog. Grandpa made a noise of disapproval in his throat when Sami interrupted to tell the time. The children cringed. Evy continued her story with a sharp look at Sami. With help from her cousins, she told about Candy finding the hat back in the clearing and finding the candy wrapper and cigarette butt on the trail.

Eli picked up the story from that point. "Then, the next day, when we rode our bikes around to the gravel road behind the farm, the same man who grabbed me showed up. He said he was looking at land to buy. I told him this was your farm and it wasn't for sale. He kept looking around, like he'd lost something."

"Probably this hat," Sami pointed at the hat that her grandfather still held in his hands.

"We figured that they were two of the guys from the bank heist in Ann Arbor," Eli continued.

"We haven't figured out where the third guy went," Evy interjected.

"We thought it would be a good plan to

search the woods at night when no one was around," Eli said. "We took Candy with us for protection. There's a small clearing toward the back of the woods. That's where we first saw the men. We found a 'possum in a hollow log, but no loot," he added.

Grandpa looked somewhat perplexed.

Evy took up the story. "That's when the man appeared. The man his friend called Jocko. The other man is called Rocky, and he's not quite as mean as Jocko. So along with our clues, we know their names, too." She paused to catch her breath. Her cousins nodded encouragement.

"Anyway, Jocko grabbed Eli. He was going to take him to the car and wanted us to come, too."

"That's when Candy bit him," Sami added.

Evy said, "She really sank her teeth into his leg. Then Eli bit him on the arm, and he let go."

"Where was the other guy?" asked their grandfather.

"On the far side of the clearing," replied Evy. "He didn't want to mess with the dog. I think he's a big chicken," she said.

"Evy had a big stick and was going to club his brains in," added Sami excitedly.

Eli said, "When the man let go of me, I ran to Evy and Sami. The bad guys went back to the road and we came to the house."

"Well," Grandpa said slowly, "you children had a close call. You know you were dis- obedient to go back there in the middle of the night, but the police will certainly benefit from your information. I believe a call to the authorities is in order." He paused a moment, thinking. "Better yet, I'll phone cousin Robbie at the State Police post. He'll know who to contact to report this." Grandpa shook his head. "Just think, bank robbers, hiding their ill-gotten loot here during their getaway."

Shortly after, the children listened on intently as Grandpa spoke with Cousin Robbie at the Jackson State Police. Robbie was actually a second cousin to their grandmother, and was always happy to hear from the family. Grandma sat nearby, lines of worry etching her face. She was quite concerned after the children shared their story again.

Robbie grew serious when Grandpa told the children's story of the attempted kidnapping and the clues they had discovered. He promised to make some calls and phone back as soon as possible.

Chapter Eighteen

Robbers Reunite

Jocko sat on the edge of the bed in the motel room and examined the deep bruise and puncture marks on the calf of his right leg. Rocky produced a first aid kit, and Jocko applied a soothing salve to his wound.

"You're lucky that big girl didn't connect with her club," Rocky offered. "Coulda' been worse."

Jocko gave his friend a withering glare and pulled his pant leg back down. There were two small rips in the material where the dog had held on.

"Boy, does this hurt," he mumbled while massaging his sore leg. Bet it's going to be stiff in the morning."

"I hope the dog has had its shots," Rocky offered.

"Oh, shut up," Jocko replied in an irritated tone. "That's all I need to worry about. Man, my arm hurts, too. Good thing I've had my tetanus booster. Now where's that Slim? He was supposed to meet us here."

As if on cue, there was a sharp rap on the door. "Get that," Jocko commanded, "but check the peep hole first. Could be the cops."

He hobbled to the apartment-sized refrigerator in one corner of the room and extracted a small bag of ice. This he applied to his sore leg.

Rocky unlatched the lock on the door and opened it to admit a smiling Slim. Rocky pumped his hand and slapped him on the back, overjoyed to see him.

"Let me take a look at that dog bite," Slim said to Jocko. "Can't be too careful with these things, you know." He stepped across the room while Jocko rolled his pant leg back up. "Not bad," Slim said observing the bruise and puncture marks. "I hope you washed it down with soap and hot water."

"Do I look stupid?" Jocko threw him a cloudy look. "Give me a break. This thing hurts like the devil," he said while rolling his pant leg back down.

"Well, what's done is done," said the always optimistic Slim. The three of us will go out bright and early tomorrow morning and find the loot. I'm not giving up on a couple of hundred thousand because of some dog and three little kids."

Rocky shook his head. "If you had seen that big girl swinging that club, you wouldn't be so sure," he said.

Slim laughed. "I've got just the thing in case we cross paths with them again." And he withdrew a can of mace from his pocket. "Some plastic zip strips will keep the kids immobile while we search," he added. "The mace is mainly for the dog. I sure don't want one of those," he said with a nod toward Jocko's leg.

Jocko grimaced as he re-applied the ice bag. "Yeah, look at this arm, too," he held it out for both to see. "The little vampire almost took it off!"

"You'll live," Slim said. "Now, let's get something to eat. I'm half starved and could really go for a pizza. I had to take a cab from Battle Creek, so I'll need the car keys to get the food."

"On the dresser," Rocky indicated. "I'll ride along if you don't mind. I'm going stir crazy here."

With a good-bye to the sore Jocko, the two men went out the door.

A half-hour later, refreshed by several slices of pizza supreme, the men finalized plans for the next morning's search. Jocko was in a better mood as he listened to Slim's account of waiting for them in the small rented apartment in Battle Creek. He had passed the last two days watching television and listening to the police scanner. Nothing was mentioned in the Battle Creek area of the search, leading Slim to feel secure in his escape.

After watching the late night news, the gang turned in for sleep. Slim stretched out on the couch. Jocko and Rocky took the beds.

Chapter Nineteen

The Interview

Detectives Bennett and Smith sat sipping the glasses of cold lemonade that Evy had brought from the house.

Bennett set his glass on the table, thanked Evy for the cold drink, and opened the thick notebook he'd produced from his brief case. The children took their places next to him at the picnic table. Their grandparents sat across from them. Candy, the farm dog lay

under the table with Puff, the cat.

"Is this the car you saw on the road

behind the farm?" He showed them a grainy

photograph from the truck stop security camera.

The children bent their heads closer.

"That's it," Eli stated. "I'm sure it's the

same car."

Evy and Sami agreed.

Detective Bennett then showed the children

pictures of three men. "The first two are

believed to be the actual robbers," he stated.

The third is thought to be the driver of the

getaway car. He was the one suspected of

burglarizing his employer's safe and obtaining

the necessary paperwork to get into the safety

deposit box."

"The first two are the guys," Evy pointed

with some tension in her voice.

"That one is Jocko," Eli touched the

picture. "He's the really bad one," he said with a shudder.

"Are these guys hardened criminals?" Grandpa asked. "Were the children in any real danger?"

"They are known to us," replied the detective, "but just for petty stuff. This is by far their biggest job. This third guy," he pointed at Slim's photo, "is believed to have provided them with the opportunity to go big time."

"We didn't see him at all," Evy said, with nods of agreement from her cousins.

"He's dropped off our radar," Bennett said. "As had these two until I got the call this morning from your cousin Robbie at the Michigan State Police post. This explains why the trail went cold at the Exit 130 truck stop." He stabbed a finger at the photograph showing the rear quarter of the Impala sedan.

"Where could they be staying?" Grandma asked. "I hope they're not camping in the area." She gave a little shiver at the thought of the crooks lingering in the neighborhood.

"After our earlier phone conversation, Smitty and I drove back to look over the vicinity south of your farm," the detective explained. "I have some officers coming tomorrow to keep an eye on the path in from the road. They'll be concealed in the woods and fields surrounding the area." He paused in thought, "We'll also start checking the local motels tonight."

"I hate to think what would have happened if Candy hadn't been with the kids," Grandma stated in a worried voice. She reached down and patted the faithful border collie while the detective nodded in agreement.

Bennett asked more questions while taking

notes. He then thanked the children for the evidence they had collected and placed his notebook back in his briefcase. "I'll be sure to let you know how things turn out," he said, smiling at the children. The detectives shook hands with Grandpa and Grandma, then with each cousin in turn. Finally, with a friendly wave and a smile, they got into the plain, unmarked car and left.

Chapter Twenty

The Trap Is Set!

Detective Bennett maneuvered the unmarked car from the freeway one exit east from Exit 130. Detective Smith rode in the passenger side. Bennett directed the car down the back roads to the gravel road that ran behind the farm. They'd been on the go since four-thirty A.M. Armed with a thermos of hot coffee and a bag of breakfast rolls, the two prepared to settle in for what could be a long wait.

"This is the lane I checked out yesterday," Bennett said to his partner as he turned the sedan off the road and shut off the headlights. Carefully driving back around the tree line, the car was shielded from view.

Meanwhile, under cover of darkness, Cousin Robbie and a fellow State Police officer were parked in their blue cruiser at the end of the farm lane on the north side of the farm. The cruiser was backed in, facing the road. The sky to the east was beginning to glow pink. Other units were concealed on the south side, around the corner from the woods.

Robbie called in their position and settled in to drink coffee from a take-out cup.

At the farm house, the three cousins eased the front door closed and crept across the drive. "We'll get one last search in before the police set up their trap," Evy said softly. "Cousin Robbie told Grandpa that they would surround the area and have police in the woods, too."

Eli said, "We'll be safe with the police around."

"I still think we should bring Candy along," Sami added. "She's been a big help."

"We don't want her giving us away," Evy replied. "Besides, she might bark at the police and reveal their position to the bad guys."

This seemed to satisfy Sami. As the trio walked through the silent barnyard to the cow pasture, they passed sleepy-eyed cattle that quietly watched them pass. They pressed on into the woods that skirted the high ground of the back pasture. Once through the barbed wire and into the deep woods, Evy stopped.

"We'll start our search more this way, further in from the road," she said.

"We didn't have any luck further back, so maybe this will pay off," said Eli. "Here's hoping this will turn something up."

"I still wish we'd brought Candy," Sami said wistfully. She shivered in the cool dampness of the late-night mist.

"Let's go," Evy said. "The police could be here at any time." And with that, she turned to walk into the woods, shining her flashlight ahead of them. The trio stopped at the first old stump they came to. The day had brightened slightly so that the trees were gray forms in the wood lot.

Eli peered into the stump. Nothing. Disappointed, the trio moved on. Eli stopped suddenly. A noise in the woods behind them caught his attention. The girls heard it, too. Evy signaled her cousins to get down.

They silently followed her lead and hid behind a thicket. As they strained their ears, they detected the sound of something stealthily moving on the path, coming from the way they had come. It was following them!

Sami stared wide eyed at her brother and cousin. The sound of something coming through the woods drew nearer. She closed her eyes tightly.

Suddenly Eli chuckled to himself.

"What on earth!" Evy said in amazement.

Sami opened her eyes to see Candy, the farm dog, standing between the crouching Eli and Evy. She busily licked their faces, her tail thrashing in delight at finding the children.

"How did she get out?" Sami asked in wonderment.

Eli shrugged his shoulders.

"Well, she's here now," Evy said. "We may

as well continue the search." She turned and crept to the next old stump. Her cousins followed along with the dog. The three cousins examined the rotted crevice. Again their search turned up empty. The next stump was a large one. Several holes from burrowing animals showed between the roots.

Candy rushed forward, sniffing around the stump and pawing at one hole in particular. Eli crouched down. He held a stick in his right hand and began vigorously probing into the depths. "Just in case there's something living in there," he said, remembering the opossum in the log. He concentrated on his search. Candy crowded in and pawed at the entrance to the burrow.

The children all knelt around the opening, intently peering in. Evy gently pulled Candy back out of the way as Eli dug around with the stick. Suddenly he threw the stick aside and plunged his arm into the hole. "Look at this!" he exclaimed, withdrawing a bundle wrapped in a brown bag.

"Let me see," Sami said, reaching for the parcel.

"There's more," Eli stated excitedly. Handing the parcel to Sami, he reached in again and produced a tin box which he handed behind him to Evy. The girls held their treasures and strained to peer over Eli's shoulder as he rested on his knees and plunged his hand in again. He felt around, then withdrew his arm. "There's nothing more," he said.

Chapter Twenty-One

Surprised!

The blue Impala sedan turned from the main road onto the gravel. The sun struggled to peek up in the east and glared into Slim's eyes. He followed Jocko's directions and guided the car to the roadside spot opposite the woods.

Slim swiveled the sun visor down to reduce the glare.

"This is it," Jocko said. Rocky agreed.

Slim shut off the engine and the men got out of the car. Jocko walked stiffly on his sore leg as Rocky led them across the ditch and through the tall, damp grass and into the woods.

Concealed in the woods some distance away, police detectives quietly called in a description of the car and the three men to Detective Bennett. On the road north of the farm, Cousin Robbie and his partner listened in. Robbie started the car. Pulling out onto the road, he headed east. He drove around the block to the south of the farm, planning to come in from the east and use his cruiser to block the road if necessary.

Meanwhile, Detectives Bennett and Smith made their way through the neighboring farm field to the north side of the wood lot.

In the woods, Rocky and Slim crept along

while Jocko limped after.

"I catch those kids again, there's going to be trouble," he groused, half to himself. His leg was stiff and throbbed painfully, and he resented having to walk on it.

Rocky led the men through the small clearing where they had conducted two prior searches. He stopped suddenly.

"Now what," Jocko muttered.

From the gloom ahead came the sounds of children's excited voices. The men listened for a moment. "They've found our loot!" Rocky whispered. His eyes grew wide with surprise.

"I just knew it," Jocko complained. "Let's go get it."

"Guess I should have come along two days ago," Slim smiled as Jocko and Rocky gave him a sullen look.

Evy had just opened the tin box as Eli and Sami examined the contents of the parcel wrapped in the cloth bag.

"I told you kids to stay away," came Rocky's harsh voice.

Startled, Evy dropped the tin box to the ground, spilling its contents of jewelry and rare coins.

The children stepped back as the three men approached. Candy, the ever-loyal farm dog, bared her teeth and advanced a step. Slim reached in his pocket for the can of mace.

Chapter Twenty-Two

The Game Is Up

Cousin Robbie parked his cruiser in front
of the blue Impala, effectively blocking it
in. A sheriff's patrol car was already behind
the car, and a deputy was getting out of the
patrol car as Robbie approached. The officer
with Robbie ran the plate number on the blue
sedan. Robbie leaned over to peer through the
Impala's windshield to record the car's

vehicle identification number.

Back at the patrol car, the Impala came up on the computer screen. The VIN number and the license plate showed the car was clean.

"A lease vehicle to a certain Thomas O'Leary," said the officer as he read the computer display. "Taken out about two months ago. Paid for in cash. There is a driver's license number and address, but they're probably fake or stolen. I'll have somebody check them out," he said.

"That figures," Robbie replied with a shake of his head.

The sudden sound of barking came from the woods, accompanied by muffled shouts. The officer got out of the patrol car and joined Cousin Robbie and the deputy in scanning the trees. Within moments, a sudden movement in the woods attracted the officers' attention. Heavy breathing of someone laboring through the brush alerted the keen senses of the policemen.

Suddenly Jocko's panting form burst from the wood lot and into the tall grass. He struggled to make progress as he was limping from the injury to his leg. The gang leader spotted the police officers and came to a sudden halt.

"Hold it right there," Robbie's partner shouted. The officer instinctively reached to unsnap his holstered firearm.

Jocko glared at the officers and bolted through the waist-high grass away from the police. The two husky police officers easily leaped the ditch and took off in pursuit of the fleeing criminal. "Stop!" Robbie shouted. "Get on the ground," he commanded while steadily gaining on the tiring Jocko.

Realizing that he couldn't outrun the athletic young State Troopers, Jocko suddenly stopped and turned to face his pursuers. Placing his hands on his head, he sank to his knees, groaning from the stiff leg that Candy had given him. The two troopers rushed through the grass and weeds and placed restraining cuffs on Jocko.

"Helloo," came a call from the woods. Detective Smith had just hustled from the tree line to discover the capture. He held a small radio communicator and spoke into it, then smiled broadly at the two State Troopers.

"The other two are prisoners of Detective Bennett and the local sheriff," he informed them. The officers grinned and nodded their approval at the news.

At this time Grandpa's white Studebaker sedan turned the corner onto the gravel road. Grandma was with him.

After marching the sullen Jocko back to the blue police cruiser, and placing him securely in the rear seat, the men turned to walk into the woods. Grandma and Grandpa got out of the Studebaker and quickly joined them.

The sound of voices and laughter echoed in the trees. Detective Bennett and several police officials led Slim and Rocky from the woods and met the others on the path through the grass. The two groups greeted each other with smiles and congratulatory hand shakes.

"We almost had them at the motel early this morning, but they had checked out moments before we got there," a sheriff was saying. "Thanks to the tips these young detectives gave us, we were hot on their trail."

"That's right," Detective Bennett put in. "They are the ones who gave us the positive I.D. and the crooks' names to crack the case wide open."

The group walked to the police cruisers.

"We'd have found the loot and been on our

way if it hadn't have been for these pesky kids," Jocko groused from the back seat of Robbie's car. "These kids, and that dog!" he forcefully added.

Candy wagged her tail and raised her head to lick at Eli's hand.

"It was the perfect job," Slim added. "If you idiots hadn't have panicked and hidden the stash, we *would* have gotten away with it."

Through the rear window, Jocko gave him a hard look.

"Where did you guys get the disguises that you used at the bank?" Detective Bennett wanted to know.

Rocky, who had been silent during the conversation, spoke up. "That was Slim's work. He had a connection with the drama department at U. of M."

"I told them I needed the disguises for a community playhouse," Slim added. "Nobody there knew anything about our plans. They didn't even know which disguises I took. That way they couldn't rat me out later." He looked dejected.

"I'd like to know how Candy got out and joined us in the woods," Evy said.

"That's easy to explain," replied Grandpa. "She was whining at the door. When she began barking, I awoke to find you kids missing. After letting Candy out, I left the house to look for you three. It was then that I ran into the good officer Patterson in the barn-yard. She had just come up from the woods, on the way to her car, and relayed the infor-mation about your safety and the gang's capture."

"It just shows that one never knows who one will run into on the farm!" Grandma added with a laugh.

Smith took up the story. "After Bennett

and I got the word that the gang was approaching the area, we walked across the field and into the wood lot. We got there just in time to see Slim, here, pull out a can of mace to use on the dog." He indicated the weary criminal with a nod of his head. "We ordered him to drop it, and then placed him and Rocky under arrest before any harm was done. Meanwhile, Jocko took off through the trees."

Detective Bennett turned to the children and smiled. "The property owner has offered a substantial reward for the recovery of the stolen items," he said. "I'll be delighted to report to him who was responsible for finding his valuables."

The children beamed broadly. Evy said, "I guess this ends the mystery of 'The Three Cousins and the Bank Heist.'"

Everyone laughed. Everyone that is, except Jocko, Rocky, and Slim.

John Riley lives with his wife, Susan, on a
small farm near Parma in rural southern
Michigan. A retired elementary teacher, John
has been writing poetry and short stories for
most of his adult life. The Three Cousins And
The Bank Heist is his second published novel.
He and Susan raised three children; one boy,
and two girls.

Besides farming and writing, John enjoys tinkering with his classic Cockshutt/Co-ops, B.F. Avery,and Minneapolis-Moline tractors and equipment. During fair weather his daily driver is a 1964 Studebaker.

Author's Note

I love to hear from my readers. Feel free to e-mail me at: rileyjohnp145@gmail.com

Sorry, I cannot respond to letters that somehow find their way to me via the U.S. Postal Service. Remember: e-mail.

www.ingramcontent.com/pod-product-compliance
Lightning Source LLC
Chambersburg PA
CBHW070943200626
46811CB00025B/894